WITHDRAWN

HUNTINGTON CITY-TOWNSHIP
PUBLIC LIBRARY
200 W. Market Street
Huntington IN 46750

Why Is This Day Special?

A Wedding

Jillian Powell

A⁺
Smart Apple Media

First published in 2005 by Franklin Watts
96 Leonard Street, London EC2A 4XD

Franklin Watts Australia
45–51 Huntley Street, Alexandria, NSW 2015

This edition published under license from Franklin Watts. All rights reserved.
Copyright © 2005 Franklin Watts

Series editor: Sarah Peutrill, Art director: Jonathan Hair, Designer: Ian Thompson, Picture researcher: Diana Morris, Reading consultant: Margaret Perkins, Institute of Education, University of Reading

Picture credits: Mark Antman/Image Works/Topham: 11t. Annie Griffiths-Belt/Corbis: 25t. Jonathan Blair/Corbis: 23. Stephen Cannerelli/Image Works/Topham: 27c. DPA/Image Works/Topham: 13t, 14, 18. Hulton Deutsch/Corbis: 19b. Hurewitz Creative/Corbis: 3. Chris Fairclough/Franklin Watts: 8b. Image Works/Topham: 4. Michael Justice/Image Works/Topham: 12. Kent Meiris/Image Works/Topham: 9b, 17t. Ray Moller/Franklin Watts: Front cover bottom, 15tr, 20b, 21tl, 21b, 22, 26t, 27t. Novosti/Topham: 24. Picturepoint/Topham: 5t. Spinning your dreams: Front cover main, 7b, 10, 15t, 19m, 25b, 26b. Zev Radovan, Israel: 13b. Zefa: 17b. Teake Zuidema/Image Works/Topham: 15b.

With thanks to the following for permission to use photographs: Spinning Your Dreams wedding photography, Russell Holdsworth, Nicola Kolndreu, Lisa Gooch, Raj and Suzannah Trivedi, and Irene Peutrill for the painting on page 8.

Published in the United States by Smart Apple Media
2140 Howard Drive West, North Mankato, Minnesota 56003

U.S. publication copyright © 2007 Smart Apple Media
International copyright reserved in all countries. No part of this book may be reproduced in any form without written permission from the publisher.
Printed in the United States of America

Library of Congress Cataloging-in-Publication Data

Powell, Jillian.
A wedding / by Jillian Powell.
p. cm. — (Why is this day special?)
Includes index.
ISBN-13 : 978-1-58340-948-0
1. Marriage customs and rites—Juvenile literature. 2. Weddings—Juvenile literature. I. Title.

GT2690.P68 2005
392.5—dc22   2005051621

9 8 7 6 5 4 3 2 1

Contents

Two people

A wedding day is often the happiest day in someone's life. It is a day he or she will always remember.

It is an important day because it is the start of a new life for two people. It joins their lives together in law, and sometimes in religion.

> *"When I grow up, I want a really big wedding with all my family and hundreds of guests! I often dream about it."*
>
> *Shobna, age 9*

When they are married, the couple usually lives together and shares everything they own. They may decide to have children.

A couple sign a register at their Christian wedding. This means that they are now married in law.

6

Some people have a quiet wedding, with just a few relatives or friends.

A couple in Borneo have a small, simple wedding with their family.

Other couples choose a big wedding with lots of guests.

The couple at this wedding chose to celebrate with a big group of friends and family.

Getting ready

Before a couple gets married, there are many things they need to do.

When the couple set a date for their wedding, they send out invitations to their family and friends.

Invitation to the wedding of Louise Burns and Peter Thomas at All Saints' Church.

If a couple chooses to have a Christian wedding, *banns* may be called in church. This means that on three Sundays, the pastor announces their wedding and asks if anyone knows of a reason why the couple may not marry.

A church official signs a certificate to say the *banns* have been read in church. This means the wedding can go ahead.

The couple chooses people who they wish to play a special part in the ceremony. There may be groomsmen and bridesmaids.

The couple will also choose their clothes and decorations, and food for the wedding feast or reception.

" I was really excited when my sister asked me to be her bridesmaid. We chose my dress together. It was in red satin. "

Lauren, age 12

A Japanese bride gets ready for her wedding.

On the big day, the bride and groom often get ready separately and see each other only at the ceremony.

Ceremonies

Weddings can have a religious or a civil ceremony.

A bride and groom follow a Christian ceremony in a church.

Many people who belong to a religion get married in a holy place such as a church, mosque, or synagogue.

In some countries, they can also have a religious ceremony in a park or garden.

"My sister was married in our mosque. It's a really special place for our family because we visit it every week."

Mina, age 8

Jewish ceremonies are held in a synagogue, park, or garden. The bride and groom may stand under a *huppah* for the ceremony.

The *huppah* stands for the home the couple will make together.

A couple are married in a civil ceremony on a beach in Mauritius.

Some people have a civil ceremony. They may get married in a public building called a registry office.

Others have a civil ceremony in a beautiful setting such as a grand house or garden, or on a beach. People can even get married at a sports stadium, in a castle, or on a submarine!

11

Vows

A very important part of a wedding ceremony is when the couple says their vows. These are promises to each other.

The couple promises to love and look after each other, and to stay together for the rest of their lives.

They say their vows in front of the wedding official and their friends and family.

" My brother was so worried that he would make a mistake when he said his vows. He practiced a lot! "

Kofi, age 8

A Muslim couple make their vows at their wedding ceremony in Malaysia.

A Hindu couple in front of a sacred fire.

In a Hindu wedding, the bride and groom say their vows as they take seven steps around a sacred fire. They say one vow with each step they take.

The marriage contract is read at a Jewish wedding in Jerusalem.

In Jewish and Muslim weddings, the couple sign a marriage contract. This sets out the rules that they will follow when they are married.

13

Tying the knot

Marriage is sometimes called "tying the knot" as two people are joined together in law and religion.

" *I went to a Hindu wedding last year. It's called Ganthibandhan when the priest ties the wedding knot.* **"**
Parvesh, age 9

In Hindu weddings, the priest ties the groom's scarf to the bride's sari to show they are joined together for life.

Then the bride and groom give each other garlands.

A Hindu couple give each other garlands made from flowers. Sometimes the garlands are made from fruit, ribbons, or beads.

In many ceremonies, the couple give each other wedding rings to show that their love will last forever. In American weddings, the groom puts the wedding ring on the third finger of his bride's left hand.

People once believed that this finger was linked to the heart.

In Orthodox Christian weddings, the couple wear crowns, which are joined together by a ribbon.

A Greek Orthodox wedding in the United States. The joining of the crowns stands for the couple's marriage.

What they wear

There are many different traditions for the clothes worn at weddings.

Color is important. In the West, it is traditional for brides to wear white as the color of purity. They sometimes wear a veil over the head.

The bride may wear the veil over her face during the ceremony. The groom lifts it over her head when they are married.

This bride is wearing a white dress and veil.

In Asia, brides often wear red, as this is the color of blood or life.

Japanese brides often wear a white kimono for the ceremony. Later they change into a brightly-colored kimono.

> **"** *My sister had lovely kimonos for her wedding because in Japan the bride changes clothes.* **"**
> *Keiko, age 8*

This bride's kimono is covered with flowers. The groom wears a traditional black kimono.

Some Sikh grooms wear a veil with a golden fringe that covers the face.

A Sikh couple exchange garlands at their wedding.

The bride

There are many old customs that people believe bring a bride good luck.

Before their wedding, Asian brides may have their hands and feet painted with *henna.*

66 *When my sister was married, we had a henna night at our house. My aunt mixed up the henna, and painted everyone's hands. I had my hands painted too.* 99

Sujata, age 8

A Muslim bride's hands decorated with *henna* for her marriage.

Flowers are carried as a bouquet or worn as garlands or in a headdress.

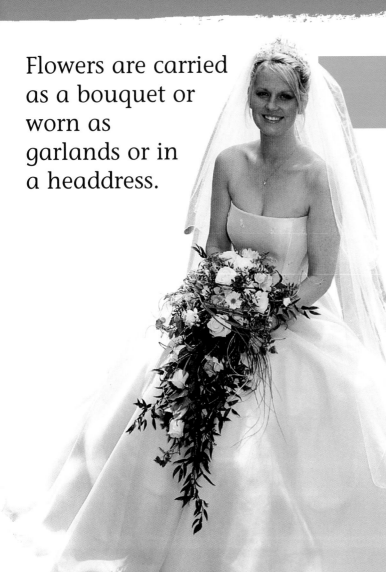

This bride has chosen a beautiful trailing bouquet.

There may be bridesmaids to help the bride. Sometimes a bridesmaid holds the train or carries the bride's bouquet.

In some Western countries, brides wear "something old, something new, something borrowed, and something blue."

In the past, some brides invited a chimney sweep to their wedding to bring good luck!

A chimney sweep wishing a bride luck in her married life, 1956.

Good luck

There are many different customs to wish a couple luck and happiness in their married life together.

At Chinese weddings, "double happiness" banners are displayed for good luck.

> 66 *At a wedding I went to, they tied horseshoes to the bride and groom's car to wish them luck when they went on their honeymoon.* 99
>
> Amy, age 9

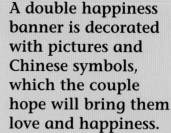

A double happiness banner is decorated with pictures and Chinese symbols, which the couple hope will bring them love and happiness.

Guests often throw rice or confetti over a couple to wish them many children.

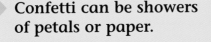
Confetti can be showers of petals or paper.

At Sikh and Hindu weddings, coconuts are given to the couple for luck.

People hope the coconuts will bring the couple a big family.

In Poland, the parents of the bride and groom give them bread and salt at the reception. The bread is so that they never go hungry. The salt reminds them that they will have hard times.

Bread and salt are given for good luck at a Polish wedding.

21

Cards and gifts

Family and friends celebrate a wedding by giving cards and gifts to the couple.

A Muslim bride and groom are given sweet foods such as dried dates.

After Muslim ceremonies, sweet foods are given to the bride and groom by each other's family to welcome them into the family.

Sometimes, a couple writes a "wedding list" of things they would like. Wedding guests can choose what to buy from the list.

The bride and groom may receive presents from their family and friends.

The wedding presents may be set out on a table at the reception for everyone to see.

A couple wears gifts of paper money at their wedding in Cyprus.

In Mexico and some European countries, guests pin money to the bride and groom for a "money dance" at the reception. This is to bring them luck and good fortune in their married life.

> " At my cousin's Sikh wedding, we all threw flower petals and gave them gifts before they went to the temple for a blessing. "
>
> Suresh, age 9

Parties and receptions

Many people celebrate weddings with a party or reception after the ceremony.

The reception may be held at a hotel, home, or other place. There are decorations, food and drink, and music for dancing. People drink toasts to wish the couple happiness.

> " *If I ever get married, I'd like a big party with lots of dancing.* "
> *Leila, age 12*

At a Russian wedding, the party is a very important part of the wedding. It can last for two days!

This Russian groom leads the dancing at his wedding reception.

This Jewish couple holds a handkerchief, which shows they have been joined in marriage.

At a Jewish wedding reception, the bride and groom sometimes sit on a chair holding either end of a handkerchief, and the guests lift them into the air.

After a wedding feast, there is often a wedding cake. The bride and groom cut the first piece of cake together to show that they are starting out on a new life as one.

A couple smiles for the camera as they cut the first slice of their wedding cake.

Remembering the day

A couple will always remember their wedding day.

Afterwards, they may send a piece of wedding cake to friends who could not go to the wedding.

There are many ways of keeping memories. Brides may keep their wedding dress or headdress, or have their wedding bouquet dried so it lasts forever.

The bride and groom can choose many types of flowers. They are a very special part of their day, which they will want to remember.

The couple may also make an album of their wedding photographs, or keep a video of the wedding.

▶ A wedding album contains treasured memories.

This couple are celebrating their diamond anniversary after 60 years together.

▲

Every year, many couples celebrate their wedding anniversary. Paper gifts are sometimes given for a first anniversary.

After 25 years, the couple celebrate their silver anniversary.

They may even reach their golden anniversary, marking 50 years together!

" My grandma and grandpa had their golden wedding anniversary last year. We had a big family party. "

Paula, age 9

HUNTINGTON CITY-TOWNSHIP
PUBLIC LIBRARY
200 W. Market Street
Huntington IN 46750

Glossary

anniversary marks the date when a wedding took place.

banns an announcement of a wedding made in church three times, to ask if there is any reason why the couple cannot marry.

best man a friend of the groom who takes care of the wedding ring.

bouquet a beautiful arrangement of flowers.

ceremony the formal part of a wedding when a couple's vows are made.

civil ceremony a wedding that is not religious.

confetti showers of paper or flower petals thrown at a wedding.

curate an assistant to a pastor in a Christian church.

custom an act that is repeated over many years.

henna a red dye made from dried leaves.

huppah a Jewish wedding canopy.

reception a feast or party held after a wedding ceremony.

registry office a building where civil weddings take place.

sacred something that is holy or blessed.

sari traditional dress for Asian women.

toast a wish for happiness or congratulations, made by raising a drink in a glass.

veil a piece of material that covers the head.

vows solemn promises.

Religions in this book

Christianity
Follower: Christian
Important figure: Jesus Christ, Son of God
God: One God as Father, Son, and Holy Spirit
Places of worship: Churches, cathedrals, and chapels
Holy book: The Bible

Hinduism
Follower: Hindu
Gods: Many gods and goddesses, including Brahma (the Creator), Vishnu (the Protector), and Shiva (the Destroyer)
Places of worship: Mandirs (temples) and shrines
Holy books: Vedas, Upanishads, Ramayana, Mahabharata

Islam
Follower: Muslim
Important figure: The Prophet Muhammad
God: Allah
Place of worship: Mosque
Holy book: The Koran

Judaism
Follower: Jew
Important figures: Abraham, Isaac, Jacob, and Moses
God: One God, the creator
Place of Worship: Synagogues
Holy Books: Tenakh, Torah, Talmud

Sikhism
Follower: Sikh
Important figure: Guru Nanak
God: One God
Place of worship: Gurdwaras (temples)
Holy book: Guru Granth Sahib

Index